This Walker book
belongs to:

For Richard

First published 2011 by Walker Books Ltd
87 Vauxhall Walk, London SE11 5HJ

This edition published 2012

2 4 6 8 10 9 7 5 3 1

© 2011 Jessica Spanyol

This book has been typeset in Typography of Coop

Printed in China

British Library Cataloguing in Publication Data:
a catalogue record for this book is available
from the British Library

ISBN 978-1-4063-3831-7

www.walker.co.uk

MY DAD *is BEAUT*iFUL

JESSICA SPANYOL

WALKER BOOKS
AND SUBSIDIARIES
LONDON · BOSTON · SYDNEY · AUCKLAND

My Dad is beautiful because
he cooks me sausages.

My Dad is beautiful because he watches cartoons with me.

My Dad is beautiful because he lets me do the watering.

My Dad is beautiful because he makes me laugh when he rides my scooter.

My Dad is beautiful because he takes me to the playground.

My Dad is beautiful because he always lets me have ice-creams.

My Dad is beautiful because he gets me comics with stickers in.

My Dad is beautiful because he is teaching me how to ride my bike.

My Dad is beautiful because
he lets me sit on his tummy.

My Dad is beautiful because he reads me books.

My Dad is beautiful because
he really loves me.

My Dad is the most beautiful
Dad in the whole world.

Jessica Spanyol has created numerous children's books, including a series about Carlo the inquisitive giraffe. She has had many different jobs as an artist – in many different places, from schools to theatres – but "Making books for children," she says, "is by far the best fun." Jessica lives in London with her husband and three children.

Other books by Jessica Spanyol:

ISBN 978-0-7445-8934-4

ISBN 978-0-7445-9491-1

The companion volume to My Dad is Beautiful...

ISBN 978-1-4063-3418-0

ISBN 978-0-7445-9831-5

ISBN 978-1-84428-512-9

Available from all good booksellers

www.walker.co.uk